For Enid, with love
J.B.

For Elijah and Joe
S.B.

First published in 2015 by Scholastic Children's Books
Euston House, 24 Eversholt Street
London NW1 1DB
a division of Scholastic Ltd www.scholastic.co.uk
London ~ New York ~ Toronto ~ Sydney ~ Auckland
Mexico City ~ New Delhi ~ Hong Kong

Text copyright © 2015 Janet Bingham
Illustrations copyright © 2015 Sebastien Braun

PB ISBN 978 1407 13945 6

Goodnight Sleepy Babies

written by Janet Bingham

illustrated by Sebastien Braun

■SCHOLASTIC

$Come$, little rabbit, it's late in the day,
Cuddle up now you're too $sleepy$ to play.
Let's watch the blue sky turn deep sunset-red,
And say $goodnight$ to the babies, ready for bed.

Goodnight baby elephant, splashing away
The dust and the heat of a tropical day.

Goodnight penguin chick, in your *comfy* seat.
You'll never feel cold on Daddy's warm feet.

Goodnight tiger cubs. Shh – don't make a peep.
It's time to *snuggle* down and wait for sleep.

Goodnight sea otter pup, *cradled* by Mummy.
You sail through the twilight, safe on her tummy.

Goodnight joey wallaby, *snuggle* up tight.
In Mummy's warm pouch you'll sleep soundly all night.

Goodnight tiny songbirds, it's time to *rest*,
Tucked up together in your treetop nest.

Goodnight little fawn, *curl up* and lie still,
Sheltered by Mummy on the moonlit hill.

Goodnight baby monkey, rocked by the breeze,
As moonbeams *dance* round the rainforest trees.

Goodnight little fox, rest your sleepy head.
Soon you'll be *snoozing* in your cosy bed.

Goodnight panda cub, give one gentle *yawn*,
Then lie sweetly dreaming till the new dawn.

Come, sleepy baby, *my own* little one,
Snug in our burrow-bed now the day's done.
The stars are bright and the moon's shining too,
And we say to each other,

"Goodnight,
I love you."